A MOUSE IN MY ROOF

A MOUSE IN MY ROOF

RICHARD EDWARDS

PICTURES BY VENICE

ORCHARD BOOKS

LONDON

Text copyright © Richard Edwards 1988
Illustrations copyright © Venice 1988
First published in Great Britain in 1988 by
ORCHARD BOOKS
10 Golden Square, London W1R 3AF
Orchard Books Australia
14 Mars Road, Lane Cove NSW 2066
1 85213 133 0

Printed in Great Britain

A MOUSE IN MY ROOF

CONTENTS

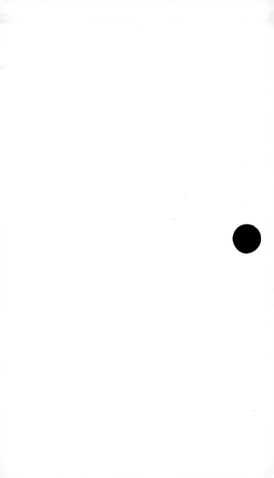

TO A MAGGOT IN AN APPLE

You lie there like a baby,
Frail and soft and curled,
I'm sorry that I broke in
To your safe white world.
I really didn't mean to,
Just blame my appetite
For laying bare your cradle
And letting in the light.
One question then I'll leave you
To slumber in the bin —
I'm feeling rather queasy,
Er . . . did you have a twin?

LOST AND FOUND

I was worrying over some homework
When my Grandad walked into the room
And sat wearily down with a grunt and a frown
And a face full of sorrow and gloom.

"I've lost it, I've lost it," he muttered,
"And it's very important to me."
"Lost what?" I replied. "I've forgotten," he sighed,
"But it's something beginning with T."

"A toffee, perhaps," I suggested,
"Or a teapot or even your tie,
  Or some toast or a thread . . ." but he shook his grey head
  As a tear trickled out of one eye.

"A tuba," I said, "or some treacle,
  Or a toggle to sew on your mac,
  Or a tray or a ticket, a tree or a thicket,
  A thistle, a taper, a tack."

But Grandad looked blank. "Well, some tweezers,
Or a theory," I said, "or a tooth,
Or a tap or a till or a thought or a thrill
Or your trousers, a trestle, the truth."

"It's none of those things," grumbled Grandad.
"A toy trumpet," I offered, "a towel,
Or a trout, a tureen, an antique tambourine,
A toboggan, a tortoise, a trowel . . ."

Then suddenly Grandad's scowl vanished,
"I've remembered!" he cried with a shout.
"It's my temper, you brat, so come here and take that!"
And he boxed both my ears and stalked out.

SAM SAID

Sam said "Do you know what's pink?
Flossie's sunburnt nose."
Sam said "Do you know what's black?
Night-time, ravens, crows."
Sam said "Do you know what's grey?
Uncle Archie's hair."
Sam said "Do you know what's white?
Brand new underwear."
Sam said "Do you know what's yellow?
Butter, sunshine, cheese."
Sam said "Do you know what's green?
Grass and pods of peas."
Sam said "Do you know what's orange?
Swedes and flames and carrots."
Sam said "Do you know what's blue?
Wings and tails of parrots."
Sam said "Do you know what's red?
Cherries, ketchup, Mars."
Sam said "Do you know what's silver?
Pins and shooting stars."
Sam said "Do you know what's purple?
Hot Ribena, plums."
Sam said "Do you know what's golden?"
"Silence," said his chums.

ON THE MOVE

Can't stop; hurry, scurrying
Underneath the day,
Got to hide myself before
The sun gives me away,
Got to find some shelter
Where the hungry hawk can't prey,
Can't stop; hurry, scurrying
Underneath the day.

Can't stop; hurry, scurrying
Underneath the night,
Got to hide myself before
The moon's too big and bright,
Got to find some shelter
Where the beastly fox can't bite,
Can't stop; hurry, scurrying
Underneath the night.

Can't stop; hurry, scurrying,
Always moving hole,
How long can I last before
This rushing takes its toll?
Wonder if in heaven
There'll be time to lounge and stroll;
One thing's sure: whoever made this world
Was not a vole.

MARY AND SARAH

Mary likes smooth things,
Things that glide:
Sleek skis swishing down a mountainside.

Sarah likes rough things,
Things that snatch:
Boats with barnacled bottoms, thatch.

Mary likes smooth things,
Things all mellow:
Milk, silk, runny honey, tunes on a cello.

Sarah likes rough things,
Things all troubly:
Crags, snags, bristles, thistles, fields left stubbly.

Mary says — polish,
Sarah says — rust,
Mary says — mayonnaise,
Sarah says — crust.

Sarah says — hedgehogs,
Mary says — seals,
Sarah says — sticklebacks,
Mary says — eels.

Give me, says Mary,
The slide of a stream,
The touch of a petal,
A bowl of ice-cream.

Give me, says Sarah,
The gales of a coast,
The husk of a chestnut,
A plate of burnt toast.

Mary and Sarah —
They'll never agree
Till peaches and coconuts
Grow on one tree.

LOOKING UPWARDS

Those big, pink faces,
Loud and round and moony,
Every time they look at me
They go completely loony;
They say "Goo-gootchie-goo,"
Or "Naughty poopsie-pooh,"
Or "Does he want his dozes?"
Or "Who's got pretty toeses?"
Or "Give his Nans a nice, wet kiss,"
Or "Give his Pops a peep,"
Or "Tickle, tickle, tum-tum," —
It's enough to make you weep.

Those big pink faces,
Teeth and gums and grins,
"Is he happy with his nappy?"
"Does he want his dins?"
They won't say dog or cow,
It's "Moo-moo," or "Bow-wow,"
And when I get a pain
It's "Windy-pops again?"
I had a thought the other day,
An awful one, that maybe
I'd grow up just as daft as them —
I think I'll stay a baby.

THE SLIVER-SLURK

Down beneath the frogspawn,
Down beneath the reeds,
Down beneath the river's shimmer,
Down beneath the weeds,
Down in dirty darkness,
Down in muddy murk,
Down amongst the sludgy shadows
Lives the Sliver-slurk;

Lives the Sliver-slurk
And the Sliver-slurk's a thing
With a gnawing kind of nibble
And a clammy kind of cling,
With a row of warts on top
And a row of warts beneath
And a horrid way of bubbling through
Its green and stumpy teeth;

With its green and stumpy teeth,
Oh, the Sliver-slurk's a beast
That you'd never find invited
To a party or a feast —
It would terrify the guests,
Make them shake and shout and scream,
Crying: "Save us from this loathesomeness,
This monster from a dream!"

It's a monster from a dream,
Haunting waters grey and grim,
So be careful when you paddle
Or go gaily for a swim:
It is down there, it is waiting,
It's a nasty piece of work
And you might just put your foot upon
The slimy Sliver-slurk.

THE BOOTS OF FATHER CHRISTMAS

We're the boots of Father Christmas
And you ought to
Give more thought to
The boots of Father Christmas
When you're merry
With your sherry,
For the boots of Father Christmas
Have a hard time
And a charred time
When the boots of Father Christmas
Land on raw coals —
Oh, our poor soles!

So the boots of Father Christmas
Ask you nicely,
But precisely:
Save the boots of Father Christmas
From our top hate —
A red hot grate,
Help the boots of Father Christmas:
When the sleigh's nigh,
Let the blaze die,
Then the boots of Father Christmas
Will be jolly
As your holly.

We're the boots of Father Christmas,
Please remember
Next December.

THE FOUR WINDS

When the wind blows from the south
It brings the sift of sands
And then I dream I'm travelling
On a camel's back through lands
Of scorpions and sphinxes
And lions on baking dunes
And palmy pools to plunge in
On white-hot afternoons.

When the wind blows from the west
It brings the wash of waves
And then I dream I'm diving
Through a maze of coral caves
Down to a sunken city
Where sharks patrol the squares
And sea-horses go trotting
Down the salty thoroughfares.

When the wind blows from the north
It brings the breath of snow
And then I dream I'm living
Like a real Eskimo
With blizzards round my igloo
And huskies round my feet
And sleds to whizz about on
And caribou to eat.

When the wind blows from the east
It brings the sigh of silk
And then I dream I'm dozing
In a bath of asses milk
While girls in baggy trousers
With cymbals on their thumbs
Do slow and snaky dances
To the thump of sleepy drums.

JUDITH

Judith, why are you kneeling on the lawn
With your ear against that little weed? What are you listening for?
Hush, says Judith, go away and leave me,
I'm waiting for this dandelion to roar.

Judith, why are you sitting in the wood
With your eyes fixed on your wristwatch? Do you want to know
    the time?
Hush, says Judith, go away and leave me,
I want to hear the bluebells when they chime.

Judith, why are you standing by that tree
With your handkerchief out ready? Come inside and go to sleep.
Hush, says Judith, go away and leave me,
I'm waiting for this willow tree to weep.

Judith, why are you lying in your bed
With some hay stalks in your left hand and some oatflakes
    in your right?
Hush, says Judith, go away and leave me,
A nightmare may come visiting tonight.

A QUERY

Oh, cabbage, oh, potato, both sizzling in one pan,
Please settle a dispute for me as quickly as you can,
I'm sorry to enquire, but it has caused me so much trouble:
Which one of you goes "squeak, squeak, squeak," and which goes
    "bubble, bubble"?

AEROBICS

Bend and stretch,
Stretch and bend,
Bend and stretch all day;
Squat down small,
Jump up tall,
What a game to play!
Though I'm young and beautiful,
I feel old and grey,
I'm sure it isn't natural
To exercise this way.

One and two,
Two and one,
One and two and three;
Up and down
Like a clown,
Oh, my aching knee!
If you want an easy life,
Take a tip from me:
A princess in a pop-up book
Is not the thing to be.

JAMES AND MRS CURRY

A carrot called James —
Yes, carrots have names —
Looked up from the veg patch and wondered
Why plump Mrs Curry
Seemed in such a hurry
As down through the garden she thundered.

Between the broad beans
And trembling greens
That shrank from her merciless stride,
She moved like an arrow
Past leek, sprout and marrow
To suddenly stop at James' side.

"I thought it looked fine,
  That boiled beef of mine,
  But no, it needs carrots," she muttered,
"At least just the one,
  Cooked briskly till done
  To a turn and then lavishly buttered."

With that she bent low
And, choosing James' row,
Grabbed hold of his feathery top,
To jump like a kitten
That thinks it's been bitten
When James cried out angrily: "Stop!

"Hands off or I'll thump you,
  I'll batter you, bump you
And, struggling as hard as I'm able,
Put up a fierce fight
With all of my might
From here to the dining - room table!"

Poor woman; what squeals!
She took to her heels
And fled away, stammering: "S - s - s - s - save me!"
And never, since then,
Served carrots again,
Just dunked soggy bread in her gravy.

NOW YOU SEE IT

I found a pot of paint
In a corner of the shed,
"To be used extremely carefully", the label said.

I found a little brush
And dipped it in the pot
And where there had been bristles, well, there suddenly were not!

I put the paint pot down
On one end of a shelf,
Up jumped our cat and spilt the paint all down her silly self

And vanished clean away
Into thin air, so now
Our Marmalade's invisible but still goes "Miaow".

It's Disappearing Paint!
Whatever can I do?
I'd pour it down the bath, but won't the bath go too?

It's Disappearing Paint,
I know that sounds absurd,
It's true though, look, I'll splosh some on this poem's last

A MOUSE IN MY ROOF

"There's a mouse in my roof!" cried Henry,
"I'll never be able to sleep,
When my weary eyes close and I'm ready to doze
That mouse starts to scamper and creep,
Or it gnaws at a beam
While I'm starting to dream,
Or it squeaks when I'm drifting away,
There's a mouse in my roof, there's a mouse in my roof!"
Poor Henry, but what can you say?

Change addresses? He did, to a new place,
Just built on the outskirts of town,
But as soon as his head touched the pillow in bed
He sat up with a "Grr!" and a frown.
Yes, you've guessed it, a mouse,
Henry stormed from the house
Yelling out till the dawn of next day:
"There's a mouse in my roof, there's a mouse in my roof!"
Poor Henry, but what can you say?

Tried hotels, tried a tent, tried a hammock,
Tried caves, tried the back of a truck,
It was all much the same, soon the scampering came
To awake him, what terrible luck!
Now he lies after dark
On a bench in the park
Bash-bash-bashing his head with a tray:
"There's a mouse in my roof, there's a mouse in my roof!"
Poor Henry, but what can you say?

35

AT THE WATERHOLE

Hysterics at the waterhole,
Guffawings in the dust:
A hundred shaggy wildebeest
Were laughing fit to bust,
Baboons, in stitches, fell about,
Slapping their hairy sides
And two young warthogs chortled till
The tears ran down their hides,
A rhino chuckled, cheetahs cheered,
Hyenas got the giggles
And one old leopard roared so much
Its spots turned into squiggles,
A hippo cooling in the pool
Yawned a gigantic grin,
While zebra-snickers, jackal-howls
And gnu-hoots joined the din,
Even a bull-frog in the mud
Sniggered a blurting croak —
And all because the elephant
Had told a human joke!

THE ROSE, THE WEED AND LUCY

The rose to the weed
Said "God had no need
To create things like you
Who have nothing to do
Except spoil
Nice clean soil."

The rose to the weed
Said "You and your breed
Are just pests on this earth
With no beauty or worth.
We grow tall
While you sprawl."

The rose to the weed
Said "Ladies take heed
Of the way that we grow,
Saying — Oh, what a show! —
But at you
They pooh-pooh."

Now, later that day
Lucy ran out to play
And was led by her nose
To the beautiful rose —
Its bright petals
And sepals,

And "Oh, you sweet bloom,
Come and perfume my room
With your scent," Lucy said
As she cut off its head —
Naughty child —
The weed smiled.

KNIGHT ERRANT

With courage in my heart
And a saucepan on my head,
I'm off to find the dragon
And to slay him till he's dead,
And when I've snuffed his flames out,
I'll chivalrously save
The poor, pale, kidnapped princess
Who is tied up in his cave.
I'll cut her cruel bonds,
I'll set her fair and free,
I'll kneel and ask respectfully
If she will marry me.
So now I boldly go
Into the wind and rain
To have that lady by my side
When I ride home again…

Well, here I am, and yes,
I took the dragon's life
And, yes, I saved the princess,
But, no, she's not my wife.
I cut her cruel bonds,
I set her fair and free,
I knelt and asked respectfully
If she would marry me,
But when I popped the question,
"You must be mad!" she said,
"To think I'd marry someone
Who puts saucepans on his head!"

SOME RESIDENTS OF RHUBARB STREET

Michelle, who lives at number 4,
Looked out one Christmas Eve and saw
A carol-singing dinosaur.
It's true, I know,
She told me so.

And Marge, who lives at number 10,
Each midnight turns into a hen,
Clucks twice and then turns back again.
It's true, I know,
She told me so.

And Fran, who lives at number 2,
Walked into church and found her pew
Swarming with sea-lions from the zoo.
It's true, I know,
She told me so.

And Luke, who lives at number 3,
Was once imprisoned in a tree
Till six woodpeckers pecked him free.
It's true, I know,
He told me so.

And as for me, I tap my feet
And say to everyone I meet:
"I love to live in Rhubarb Street."
It's true, I do,
Well, wouldn't you?

LONELY VIOLET

Lonely Violet wept for years
On her misty Highland hill,
Tears and tears and tears and tears,
Buckets of them, floods, until
All her rooms were waterlogged,
Everything so soaked and sogged
That the rising tide of water
Trapped the Highlands' hapless daughter
Up inside the tiny loft
Of her overflowing croft.

Luckily a local laddie,
Known as something of a loon,
Jolly James McGilliegaddy,
Joker, comic, clown, buffoon,
Heartiest of Highland hearties,
Life and soul of Highland parties,
In the nick of time rode by,
Cracked a joke and rescued Vi
From her wet and wobbly rafter
With a ladder made of laughter…

They lived happily ever after.

TEN TALL OAKTREES

Ten tall oaktrees
Standing in a line,
"Warships," cried King Henry,
Then there were nine.

Nine tall oaktrees
Growing strong and straight,
"Charcoal," breathed the furnace,
Then there were eight.

Eight tall oaktrees
Reaching towards heaven,
"Sizzle," spoke the lightning,
Then there were seven.

Seven tall oaktrees,
Branches, leaves and sticks,
"Firewood," smiled the merchant,
Then there were six.

Six tall oaktrees
Glad to be alive,
"Barrels," boomed the brewery,
Then there were five.

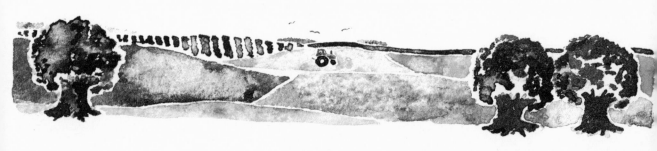

Five tall oaktrees,
Suddenly a roar,
"Gangway," screamed the west wind,
Then there were four.

Four tall oaktrees
Sighing like the sea,
"Floorboards," beamed the builder,
Then there were three.

Three tall oaktrees
Groaning as trees do,
"Unsafe," claimed the council,
Then there were two.

Two tall oaktrees
Spreading in the sun,
"Progress," snarled the by-pass,
Then there was one.

One tall oaktree
Wishing it could run,
"Nuisance," grumped the farmer,
Then there were none.

No tall oaktrees,
Search the fields in vain,
Only empty skylines
And the cold grey rain.

THE WAVES

I stood for a long, long time,
Watching the surf race in
And wondering which of Nature's laws
Made all those waves begin.
Why did the breakers break?
And why did the rollers roll?
Why didn't the sea just slop about
Like soup in a great big bowl?

To find the answer out
I called on my Uncle Joe,
Who knows more facts about this earth
Than anyone else I know.
"Aha!" he said, "the waves!
You were right to come to me,
I'm one of the few chaps in the world
Who's solved that mystery."

"It's nothing to do with the wind,
Or the fact that the earth's not flat,
There's a much more extraordinary reason why
The sea behaves like that,
And I'll tell you about it now
If you cross your heart and you swear
To never tell anyone else in your life."
And I did and I haven't. So there!

DASHING AWAY

One crease said to another crease
"Quite soon we won't exist."
They sobbed and wrinkled closer
And delicately kissed,
And side by side lay bravely
While Betty, with a frown,
Spread out her new washed jeans
And brought the steam iron down.

OH, TO BE...

"Oh, to be an eagle
 And to swoop down from a peak
 With the golden sunlight flashing
 From the fierce hook of my beak.

"Oh, to be an eagle
 And to terrify the sky
 With a beat of wings like thunder
 And a wild, barbaric cry.

"Oh... but why keep dreaming?
 I must learn to be myself,"
 Said the rubber duckling sadly
 On its soapy bathroom shelf.

BEHIND THE WATERFALL

There's a cave behind the waterfall,
A green stream-curtained cell,
It's hidden by a fringe of ferns
But Tarzan knows it well
And when the cruel white-hunter gang
Is hard on Tarzan's trail,
He slips in through the close cascade
And hides behind its veil.

There's a cave behind the waterfall
And in it Tarzan's stock
Of things all forest dwellers need
Is piled on shelves of rock:
Spare loincloths, jars of jungle wine,
Rare aromatic roots,
The antidote for python bites,
Heaped trays of oozy fruits.

There's a cave behind the waterfall
Where Tarzan likes to lie,
Head pillowed on a crocodile
While owls and nighthawks cry,
And sometimes, when a rising moon
Shines sparkling through the fall
And turns the water into ropes
Of pearls, Jane comes to call.

There's a cave behind the waterfall
And if you ever go
Away, by vine, on jungle business,
Tarzan, let me know,
I'll swim the seas to Africa
And guard your cave with pride
Till you and Jane splash home again
With Cheetah by your side.

A WORD IN YOUR EAR

Those people who have one large ear
And one that's very small should fear
Being caught out in a sudden gale
For then the large ear, like a sail,
Could trap the wind and whirl them round
Until they drilled into the ground
And, spinning like a giant top,
Came only slowly to a stop
When somewhere near Australia. So
If you have one large ear, please go
Outside with care, avoid strong breezes,
Keep away from outsize sneezes
Or, to save all this palaver,
Wear a well-made Balaclava.

RECOLLECTIONS OF AN OLD SPOOK

Quite a posh old house was this,
Years and years ago,
Red fires crackled in the hearths
Where now tongues of snow
Poke down broken chimney pots
When the rude winds blow.

Quite a posh old house was this,
Solid, waterproof,
Keeping all its gentlefolk
Sheltered and aloof,
Now the common sparrows squat
Cheeping in the roof.

Quite a posh old house was this,
Full of chinless earls
Dressed in frilly shirts of silk
Chasing silly girls
While the powdered chaperones
Twiddled with their pearls.

Quite a posh old house was this,
Now nobody cares,
Perhaps it's just as well to lose
All those snobby airs,
Still, I did enjoy myself:
Haunting down the stairs,

Chasing Lady Otterbourne,
Making Lord Snoot shriek,
Kissing, quite invisibly,
Rosie's rosy cheek —
Now it's just a wandering rat
If the floorboards creak.

Time for me to make a move,
Find a newer place,
Somewhere more appreciative
Of my ghostly grace,
Somewhere snug and double-glazed
With less draughty space.

Where though? Perhaps a penthouse flat
With a city view,
Perhaps a bed-sit, perhaps a pub,
Even digs would do,
Anywhere that's…unpossessed…
Perhaps I'll call on
You!

BRAMBLE TALK

A caterpillar on a leaf
Said sadly to another:
"So many pretty butterflies…

I wonder which one's Mother."

FIGBERT JIFFY

What's that rumour? What's that clack?
Figbert Jiffy's coming back!
Figbert Jiffy? Are you sure?
Have you warned the Crocador?
Put away those noises, run,
Tell Pantucket what's begun,
Stuff all shadows in one sack:
Figbert Jiffy's coming back!

Boil that kettle! Chomp that snack!
Figbert Jiffy's coming back!
Figbert Jiffy? Ask Tout-Tout
If he's snuffed the cold fires out,
Anywhere a lunx can fit
Shoo one in and stand by it,
Notify the natterjack:
Figbert Jiffy's coming back!

Zip that waistcoat! Belt that mac!
Figbert Jiffy's coming back!
Figbert Jiffy? Light Dark Lane,
Let the Quiet Man speak again,
All along the snaky stream
Things like saucepans clank and steam,
Things like ducks go quack, quack, quack!
Figbert Jiffy's coming back!

THE ONCE-A-CENTURY WORM

A quiet wood, a scratching sound from underneath a bush,
I ran to look; the leaf-mould quaked, then gave an upward push
And, gaping as it surfaced in that dim and shady place,
A worm emerged, a worm that wore a tiny human face.

"I am the Once-A-Century Worm," it squeaked, "and we are rare,
For only every hundred years we need a gulp of air,
And when we've gulped that gulp we disappear back underground
To doze and dream before another century comes round."

With that it closed its eyes and stretched its little worm-mouth
        wide,
Breathed in until a century's worth of air was safe inside,
And then sank out of sight, while in its place a worm-cast curled —
But what's a common worm-cast to convince this doubting world?

So now I take a camera with me everywhere I go
And crawl around on hands and knees beneath the bushes, so
If I should see another one, a photo will confirm
The strange (but true) existence of the Once-A-Century Worm.

USELESS THINGS

A spout without a hole
A Swiss without a roll
Ladders without rungs
Taste without tongues,

A shepherd without sheep
A horn without a beep
Hockey without sticks
Candles without wicks,

A pier without the sea
A buzz without a bee
A lid without a box
Keys without locks,

A harp without a string
A pong without a ping
A broom without its bristles
Refs without whistles,

A glacier without ice
Ludo without dice
A chair without a seat
Steps without feet,

A hat without a head
A toaster without bread
A riddle without a clue
Me without you.

UPS AND DOWNS

A kangaroo, who was leaping about
In the outback way down under,
Kept bouncing her baby out of her pouch,
"Stap me!" said she. "What a blunder
For kangaroo sheilas like me to be made
Like this — what a duffo slip —
To give us such bonzer pouches and then
To forget the flaming zip!"

MUDGE

I'm Mudge,
That's me,
I'm the one
You cannot see,
I'm the space
Between the floor
And the bottom
Of a door,
I'm the small hole
In your shoe
Which the rain
Comes leaking through,
I'm Mudge,
That's me,
I'm the one
You cannot see.

I'm Mudge,
That's me,
I'm the one
You cannot see,
I'm the puncture
In a wheel,
I'm the cleft
That grabs a heel,
Lift a drain:
I'm there beneath,
I'm the gap
Between your teeth

That permits
A piercing whistle
Or may trap
A piece of gristle,
In a bath
You plug me, so
I peep through
The overflow,

In a wall
I'm that dark crack,
You may fill me,
I'll be back,
I'm the one
You'd like to banish
But you can't
Make vanish vanish,
I was here
Before the birth
Of your bright
And spinning earth,
I'll be there
My solid friend,
When the world
Comes to an end,
I'm Mudge,
That's me
I'm the one
You cannot see.

THE SHELLFISH RACE

"Are they ready?" asked the flounder, who'd agreed to referee
 At the bottom of the Channel just off Angmering On Sea.
"Are you ready?" asked the starter, a pernickety old dab.
"Yes, I'm ready," lisped the lobster. "Yes, I'm ready," croaked the crab.
"Yes, I'm ready," piped the prawn, "although I've got an awful limp."
"Yes, I'm ready," called the crawfish. "Yes, I'm ready," squeaked
       the shrimp.

"On your marks," the starter bubbled: on their marks the shellfish got,
 Then a flag-like fin was lowered and away the athletes shot
 Down a running track so murky and so tangled up with weed
 It was difficult to know which one had surged into the lead;
 But the lobster beat the crawfish by a short claw to the post
 And the sound of fishy cheering echoed up and down the coast.

Third to finish, with a flourish of its feelers, was the shrimp,
 Closely followed by the puffed-out prawn, remembering to limp;
 Then they ran a lap of honour round a boulder in the bay
 Before marching off together in a most unshellfish way
 To get ready for the revels of the celebration dance —
 All except the sideways-scuttling crab who ended up in France.

? ? ?

"I've lately discovered," the Prof. said to Ron,
"That monkeys are people with overcoats on."
"But how do you know," answered Ron to the Prof.
"That people aren't monkeys with overcoats off?"

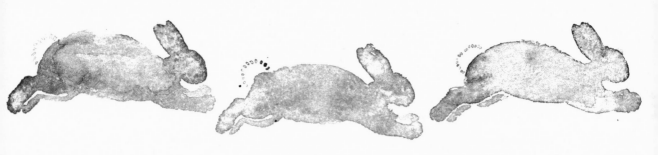

PERCY POT-SHOT

Percy Pot-Shot went out hunting,
Percy Pot-Shot and his gun,
Percy Pot-Shot, such a hot shot,
Shot a sparrow, said "What fun!"

Percy Pot-Shot shot a blackbird,
Shot a lapwing, shot a duck,
Shot a swan as it rose flapping,
Shot an eagle, said "What luck!"

Percy Pot-Shot shot a rabbit,
Shot a leaping gold-eyed hare,
Shot a tiger that lay sleeping,
Shot a rhino, shot a bear.

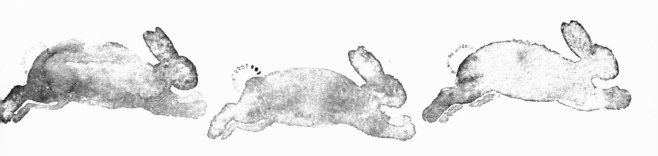

Percy Pot-Shot, trigger happy,
Shot a fountain, shot a tree,
Shot a river, shot a mountain,
Shot some rainclouds, shot the sea.

Percy Pot-Shot went on hunting,
Percy Pot-Shot and his gun,
Not a lot that he had not shot,
Shot the moon down, shot the sun.

Percy Pot-Shot stood in darkness,
No bird fluttered, no beast stirred,
Percy Pot-Shot knelt and muttered
"God forgive me." No one heard.

TO PASS THE TIME

When I'm bored I count things:
Cornflakes, cars,
Pencils, people, leaves on trees,
Raindrops, stars,
Footsteps, heartbeats, pebbles, waves,
Gaggles, herds and flocks,
Freckles, blinks per minute,
The ticks
Of clocks.

Eighty-seven lamp-posts
Line our street.
Did you know a woodlouse has
Fourteen feet?
And — three vests, four pairs of pants, six shirts, two
T-shirts, one pair of jeans, two other pairs of trousers,
one pair of shorts, two belts, three pullovers (one of
them without sleeves), a raincoat, a jacket, two pairs
of pyjamas, one glove, one tie and eleven socks are
The clothes I've got
In five drawers and one wardrobe:
I'm bored
A lot.

FLORINDA MACKINTOSH

Freddie Bangle's up a ladder,
Linda Loop is in her room,
Oswald Knutt is ambling back from school,
Rose O'Lummy's playing hopscotch,
Ian Tot's in Thailand,
Nigel Snoot, the first, is at the pool,
Dawn Maracca's in the doghouse,
Annie Junket's with her aunt,
Mildred Pea's been yodelling for hours,
Arthur Weasel's in the bathtub,
Clarence Vat's in Venice,
Kate Van-Handle's outside painting flowers,
Iris Eel is walking Rover,
Nelly Jelly's picking pears,
Thisbee Foot has found a tree to climb,
Olly Hump's in Oslo,
So where's Florinda Mackintosh?
Hidden in the letters of this rhyme.

THE THING EXTRAORDINAIRE!

Oh, you should have been there
Listening to the whizz
Of curtains opening and the sudden blare
Of someone's voice announcing:
"Kiddies, here he is —
Half man, half beast — The Thing Extraordinaire!"

Oh, you should have been there,
Oh, you should have seen
His tusks, his plume, his fur, his twisted hat,
The way when, walking upright,
He always seemed to lean,
His shadow slinking round him like a cat.

Oh, you should have been there,
Oh, you should have heard
The gruff and ghostly grunting from his snout,
His burble like a geyser,
His whistle like a bird,
The swish-swosh as he waved his tail about.

Oh, you should have been there,
Oh, you should have known
The thrill that filled us when we watched him dance:
His arms flung up like antlers,
His feet clumped down like stone,
His silver eyelids flickering in a trance;

Then he sort of shimmered
And seemed to haze away,
He faded... but that's not quite what I mean...
Exactly how he vanished
I'm not prepared to say —
You should have been there, oh, you should have been!

HOLIDAY HILL

Oh, for a bottle
Oh, for a plum
Oh, for a pie
And a crust with a crumb
Oh, for a salad
Oh, for a spoon
Oh, for a laze
And a hot afternoon
Oh, for a hillside
Oh, for a rug
Oh, for a straw
And some juice in a jug
Oh, for a sausage
Oh, for a dip
Oh, for a crisp
And a grape with a pip
Oh, for a sundae
Oh, for a slice
Oh, for a bowl
And a raspberry ice.

Oh, for a catnap
Oh, for a sigh
Oh, for a moth
And a bat in the sky
Oh, for a sunset
Oh, for a pack
Oh, for a yawn
And a slow saunter back
Oh, for an owl-hoot
Oh, for a thrill
Oh, for a picnic
On Holiday Hill.

ME AND HIM

"What did you do when you were young?"
  I asked of the elderly man.
"I travelled the lanes with a tortoiseshell cat
  And a stick and a rickety van,
  I travelled the paths with the sun on a thread,
  I travelled the roads with a bucket of bread,
  I travelled the world with a hen on my head
  And my tea in a watering can,"
Said the elderly, elderly man.

"And what do you do now that you're old?"
  I asked of the elderly man.
"I sit on my bed and I twiddle my thumbs
  And I snooze," he replied, "and I plan
  To make my escape from this nursing-home place
  Whose matron is strict with a pale pasty face..."
"Then come with me now and away we shall race!"
  I said to the elderly man
  And he jumped out of bed and we ran.

  And now we wander wherever we want,
  Myself and the elderly man,
  With a couple of sticks and a tortoiseshell cat
  And a rickety-rackety van,
  We travel the paths with the sun on a thread,
  We travel the roads with two buckets of bread,
  We travel the world with a hen on each head
  And our tea in a watering can,
  Young me and the elderly man.

EUGENIE AND THE ICE

It grew cold. Puddles froze
And the wind like a knife
Swept out of Siberia
Chilling the life
Of the blackbird, the starling,
The sparrow, the crow,
And burying fields
Under blank sheets of snow.

It grew colder. The streams
Turned as solid as stone,
White waterfalls fanged
As if carved out of bone.
The wagtail, the moorhen,
The dipper all flew
To feed by the sea —
Then the sea froze too.

"It's *too* cold!" said Eugenie,
And marching outside
She strode down to the edge
Of the desolate tide,
Where she faced the cruel wind
With a shake of her fist,
Shouting: "Shoo! Scram! Skidaddle!
Buzz off! I insist!"

Well, the wind didn't wait
To be shouted at twice,
It turned tail and fled home
While, in place of the ice,
Water warmed, water woke,
Water gurgled and gushed,
Water spouted and sparkled
And rippled and rushed.

And the birds! How they sang!
From the heron's sharp bill
Came a croak of delight,
From the wren came a trill,
And a turtle dove purred
On each branch of each tree
As Eugenie walked home
From the blue-again sea.

A DAY IN SPRING

I was lying in the bath
With the squidgy soap at hand
When a shout came from the garden:
"It's coming in to land!
It's saucer-shaped, it's huge,
It's come from outer space!
There's something at the porthole:
A hand? A foot? A face?
It's gliding past the roof,
It's hovering silently,
And now the hatch is opening…
Whatever can *that* be?
Six arms, four legs, a tail,
A head shaped like a bell,
It's floating down towards me,
Oh, no!"… then silence fell.

I slithered through the suds,
I splashed out of the tub,
I wrapped a towel around me,
No time for rub-a-dub,
I hurried to the window,
I clambered on a stool,
I looked down at… my brother
Grinning upwards: "April Fool!"

ROSE ROSE

Rose Rose is her name and her colour,
Her favourite colour, is pink:
Pink cushions, pink curtains, pink crayons,
Pink envelopes, even pink ink.

She bathes in a salmon-pink bathtub,
She dreams between pink satin sheets,
She wriggles her toes in pink slippers,
Pink prawns are her favourite eats.

Pinks crowd every bed in her garden,
Each shrub bears a coral-pink bloom,
Pink vases of pink cherry blossoms
Pink-perfume her pink-papered room.

Each evening at blushing-pink sunset
She climbs to the top of Pink Hill
And closing her eyes, facing westwards,
Thinks pink and thinks pinker until

Pink wings like the wings of flamingos,
Unfurl from her shoulders and raise
Rose Rose off her feet towards heaven…
So come to the window and gaze:

Gaze out at Rose Rose as she circles,
Gaze out at Rose Rose as she flies,
Gaze out at Rose Rose as she tumbles and drifts
Down the fiery pink paths of the skies.

I LIKE IT HERE

I like being here, beside this lazy river,
I like it in these shallows where the reed tips quiver,
I like the way the minnows nudge for breadcrumbs from my hand,
I like to squirm my toes and send up little smokes of sand.

I like being here when the swan drifts by
With a ruffle of her feathers and a glitter of her eye,
I like the ducks, the plopping frogs, the dragonflies, the trout,
Whose sudden silver splashes make my shadow dance about.

I like being here, with all these watery things,
Who don't waste time with telling tales or silly gossipings,
And don't care if I'm rich or poor or fat or dim or clever,
I like being here; I think I'll stay for ever.